For Mimi, Zen, Stan and Ember – B. F.

For Helen and the family – B. C.

Bloomsbury Publishing, London, Oxford, New York, New Delhi and Sydney

First published in Great Britain in 2016 by Bloomsbury Publishing Plc
50 Bedford Square, London WC1B 3DP

www.bloomsbury.com

BLOOMSBURY is a registered trademark of Bloomsbury Publishing Plc

A CIP catalogue record for this book is available from the British Library

ISBN 978 1 4088 6719 8 (HB)
ISBN 978 1 4088 6720 4 (PB)
ISBN 978 1 4088 6718 1 (eBook)

All papers used by Bloomsbury Publishing are natural, recyclable products made
from wood grown in well managed forests. The manufacturing processes
conform to the environmental regulations of the country of origin

Printed in Italy by Graphicom

1 3 5 7 9 10 8 6 4 2

WATCH OUT FOR Muddy Puddles!

Written by **Ben Faulks**

Illustrated by **Ben Cort**

BLOOMSBURY

LONDON OXFORD NEW YORK NEW DELHI SYDNEY

Watch out for muddy puddles . . .

because you never really know,
what there might be lurking
down in the depths below!

You see, puddles can be hiding
so many different things . . .

long-lost footballs,
lonely socks
and underwater kings.

But not all muddy puddles
are completely
danger-free . . .

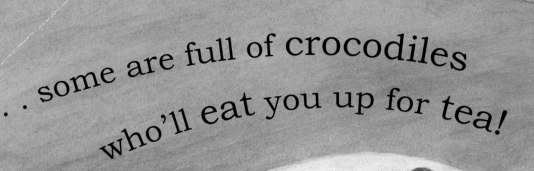

. . . some are full of crocodiles
who'll eat you up for tea!

And tell me, have you ever
been taken puddle fishing?

Look – angry pirates, giant squid
and – yeuch! – two
frogs a-kissing!

Then this one,
   for example,
is the frozen, icy kind.
Tread with care.

Watch out! Don't slip . . .
      too late –
         a sore
            behind!

Sometimes on the surface
a puddle may look intriguing . . .

just mind your step,
watch out –
BEWARE!
Looks can be deceiving!

Some puddles will spin you round and round

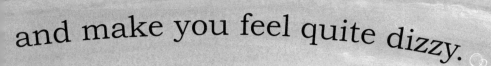
and make you feel quite dizzy.

Just like a giant whirlpool –
all *twisty*,
whirly,
whizzy.

Others, they are deep.

How deep? You cannot tell.

But one thing is for sure –

if you jump in, it's farewell.

Aaargh!

You'll sink and sink
and go straight down –
straight down through
the planet . . .

tumbling past the
sandstone,
the fossils
and the
granite.

But the puddle that's by far the worst
(that's if you're dead unlucky),
is the one that's home sweet home
to the BIG BAD rubber ducky!

He's fearsome and he's yellow,
so tiptoe, be discreet.
If you disturb the waters,
he'll chase you
down the street.

Though if you're brave – just splash around,

puddles are
great fun!

Splishy splashy silliness, enough for . . .

. . . everyone!

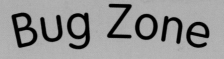

Bug Zone

Bug Athletes

Barbara Taylor

Chrysalis Children's Books

First published in the UK in 2003 by
Chrysalis Children's Books
An imprint of Chrysalis Books Group Plc
The Chrysalis Building, Bramley Road, London W10 6SP

Paperback edition first published in 2005

Copyright © Chrysalis Books Group Plc 2003
Text by Barbara Taylor.

ISBN 1 84138 815 7 (hb)
ISBN 1 84458 265 5 (pb)

British Library Cataloguing in Publication Data
for this book is available from the British Library.

Editorial manager: Joyce Bentley
Assistant editor: Clare Chambers

Project manager and editor: Penny Worms
Designer: Angie Allison
Picture researcher: Jenny Barlow
Consultant: Michael Chinery

Printed in Hong Kong
10 9 8 7 6 5 4 3 2 1

Words in bold can be found in the glossary on page 30.